Musings of a Restless Heart

REi AGUSTIN

Ukiyoto Publishing

All global publishing rights are held by

Ukiyoto Publishing

Published in 2024

Content Copyright © REi AGUSTIN

ISBN 9789362698056

All rights reserved.
No part of this publication may be reproduced, transmitted, or stored in a retrieval system, in any form by any means, electronic, mechanical, photocopying, recording or otherwise, without the prior permission of the publisher.

The moral rights of the author have been asserted.

This is a work of fiction. Names, characters, businesses, places, events, locales, and incidents are either the products of the author's imagination or used in a fictitious manner. Any resemblance to actual persons, living or dead, or actual events is purely coincidental.

This book is sold subject to the condition that it shall not by way of trade or otherwise, be lent, resold, hired out or otherwise circulated, without the publisher's prior consent, in any form of binding or cover other than that in which it is published.

www.ukiyoto.com

Dedication

To God who has blessed me with this life full of endless possibilities.
To my son and family who serve as anchors that keep me grounded.
To my best friends in the world who never grow tired of listening, cheering me up, reminding me that I am magical and that I should receive the love I deserve.
To all of my past loves, thank you for the lessons and experiences that served as inspiration.
To the one I hold dear to my heart, thank you for your trust and your love.

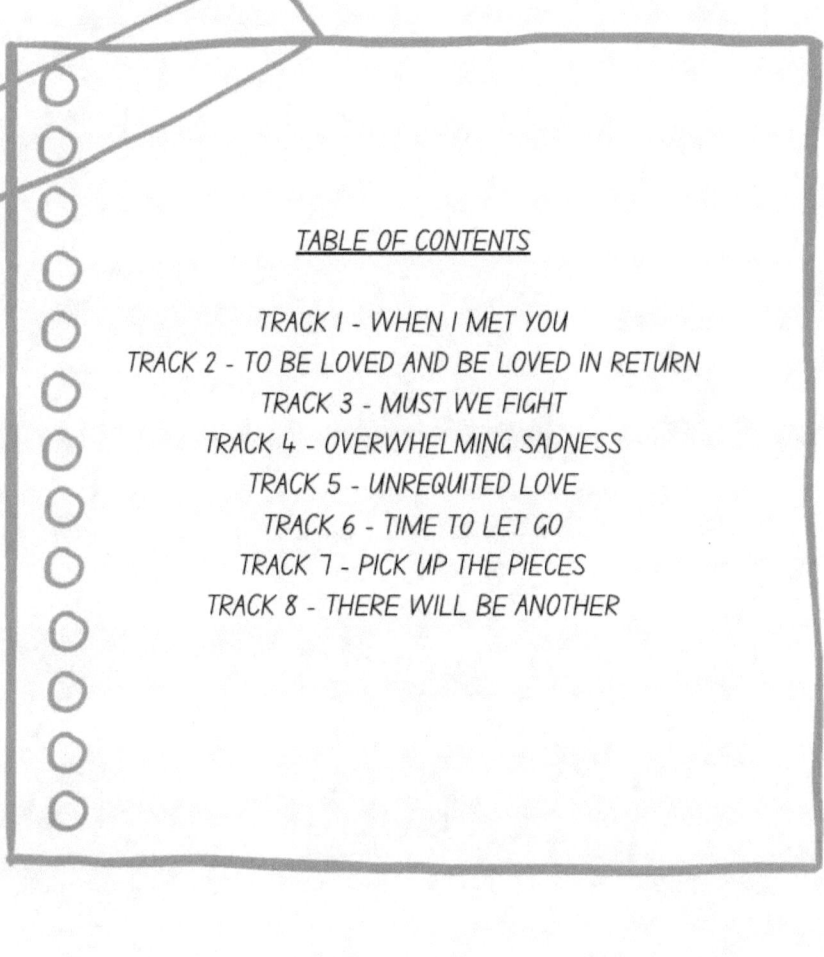

TABLE OF CONTENTS

TRACK 1 - WHEN I MET YOU
TRACK 2 - TO BE LOVED AND BE LOVED IN RETURN
TRACK 3 - MUST WE FIGHT
TRACK 4 - OVERWHELMING SADNESS
TRACK 5 - UNREQUITED LOVE
TRACK 6 - TIME TO LET GO
TRACK 7 - PICK UP THE PIECES
TRACK 8 - THERE WILL BE ANOTHER

SYNOPSIS

How do I begin? A prologue by definition is "a story before the story". This book is not a novel, but it can tell a story. What about you say? What else but the most powerful emotion there is on the planet? Love.

"Musings of a Restless Heart" is a collection of poems, quotes, and write-ups on finding love, losing it, moving on, and doing it all over again. Our experiences may differ in nature, but these writings may elicit the same emotions.

This compilation talks about love and its many facets -- Friendships formed that caught on fire, quiet understandings, enraged misreadings, beautiful mistakes, exaggerated reactions, petty misunderstandings, wrongful interpretations, and differing beliefs.

Through the years, in bouts of intense emotions, I would watch movies, read novels, and write. While writing, I listened to songs that would fuel my feelings.

Reading through this randomness now makes me laugh at how dramatic I can get, teary-eyed remembering the pain and what-ifs, and relieved that I got out of unsuitable situations in one piece! I remember the people involved – The man, and the poor friends who endured listening for hours (even years!) on how I can fall too fast and feel too much.

As you read through the pages, I hope you also get to remember --- A person, a feeling, a situation. Just remember, good or bad, you've experienced them and has made you who you are today.

NOTE: Some are written in Filipino. Emotions are best expressed in one's first language.

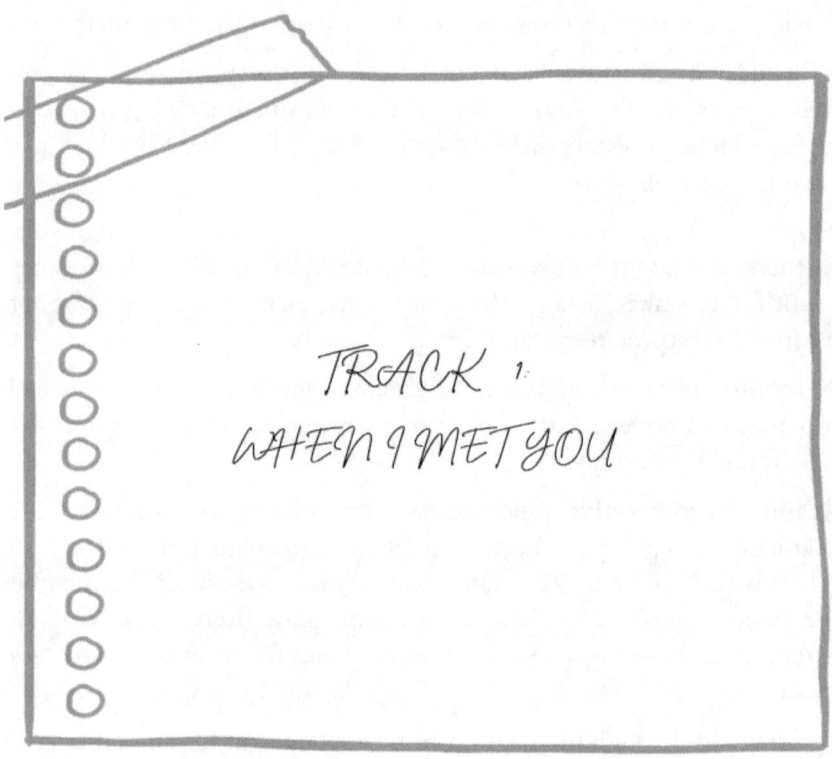

Playlist Companion

So It's You by Raymond Lauchengco

When I Met You by Apo Hiking Society

The Search Is Over by Survivor

Please Be Careful with My Heart by Jose Mari Chan

Afraid for Love to Fade by Lea Salonga

A Very Special Love by Sarah Geronimo

I'm Yours by Jason Mraz

Love Is All Around by Wet Wet Wet

Every Second by Mina Okabe

Loving You by Ric Segretto

"Ready? Dive!"

They say you don't go looking for love. It finds you. It will come at the right time when you are ready.

How do we know though that we're ready? Is it through the number of days, months, and years waiting? Is it through manifestations of self-love?

More importantly, how do we know it's love when it comes?

I guess we'll never really know. What we can do is just to jump right in and have faith in each other that if it's love, it will persist. Both should accept that love is a mutual understanding between souls and that love is a work in progress.

"I dream of a love that even time will lie down and be still for."

- Practical Magic

Love to me is more
Than just a feeling in the spring
Or the warm loving feeling
That the though of you can bring
Love is more than all the special things
I can't seem to count about you
It's more than just the loneliness
That I feel when I'm without you
Love is more than all these things
In fact, the whole year through
At any time and all the time
Love to me is you.

When you know, you just know…

I know a smile I love to see
A voice I love to hear
I know a hand I love to hold
A presence I love to be near
I know a heart, a loving heart
That's thoughtful, pure and true
I know them all and love them all
For they belong to you.

"Never go in search of love, go in search of life, and life will find you the love you seek."

Our first times
Are the ones I remember the most
The first time we met
The first time we talked
The first time you called
And we went out
The first time that we were separated
And I told you I'd miss you
The first time I cried when you were gone
The first time you told me
The first time I said I love you
And the time you loved me back
The first time I met your family and friends
The first time that you met mine
And the first time that I knew
Our love was going to last
There have been many first times
Each of them unforgettable
And it's comforting to know
There'll be a lifetime of first with you.

"I believe lahat tayo may soulmate. Kahit anong takas ng kaluluwa mo, dadalhin at dadalhin ka pabalik dun sa soulmate mo."

I miss you…
Maybe because of your looks
And maybe because you care
Maybe because you have your ways
Of making our times happier
Maybe because of the way you talk
Especially when we're together
Maybe because you kid around
Or maybe because you're serious
I miss you…
Maybe because I feel something
That is not worth denying
It's a feeling you don't even know
'cause I'll never ever tell or show
Maybe because you're such a part of me
Or maybe because you sometimes hurt me
But whatever it is I keep on thinking about it
It plays with my mind and I'm starting to regret it
But maybe it's true
That I feel something for you
Maybe I do love you.

TRACK 2:
To Be Loved and Be Loved In Return

Playlist Companion

You by The Carpenters

Dear by Ben & Ben

Paninindigan Kita by Ben & Ben

Uhaw by Dilaw

Kahit Maputi na ang Buhok Ko by Rey Valera

I Love You Too Much by Diego Luna

No Arms Can Ever Hold You by Chris Norman

We and Us by Moira Dela Torre

A Love To Last a Lifetime by Sarah Geronimo

Perfect by Ed Sheeran

"Love Wins"

> "Did I ever really love Big, or was I addicted to the pain? The exquisite pain, of wanting someone so unattainable?"

Oh Carrie...Such words of wisdom that I will never grow tired of hearing. You never fail to make me think, rethink and wonder.

This goes out to all who are going through unrequited love. Maybe, just maybe, it's not really love, but just an addiction of going after what you can't have.

Although...who wouldn't want to be like Carrie (fashion included)? She ended up with Big after all.

> **"We have a good story to tell. The question is, after the happiness...What now?" – OM**

All great relationships have good stories to tell. I guess the challenge is sustainability. After everything has been done, after magical moments were collected, after making things work, keeping it at that level or improving is what makes it challenging and requires more hard work.

Doing everything right in making things work is never enough. There should be dedication and commitment to do so. Yes, you may be happy, but what happens when that happiness is not sustained? What if unforeseen circumstances happen and that happiness is tampered? Do you hold on or let go of the idea that you can still make things better? Is your heart still set on making things work, or do you quit and walk away?

Commit to something to set direction.

"I noticed that you always want your drink sweeter than usual." – Barista

Yes, I do. In almost everything that I do, I make it a point that it's never "the usual". There always must be that "extra" to make moments more meaningful, more magical.

With customer service, you have to go the extra mile. Being in the same industry my entire career, it is but natural that I have applied the same principle in day-to-day situations as well.

It won't hurt to put in a little extra out there. It will make people remember you. And who knows, to that person you show some extra of something to, you may have given their day that sugar rush it needs to get them going.

"Wasted Time"

"Never let the same person waste your time twice." - IG

Or more than twice.

But what if the time you're wasting with that person is worth it? What if both of you are enjoying wasting each other's time? Is it still a waste? Is everything just a matter of perspective?

I'd say, life is short. Do what makes you happy. If wasting time with him is one of them, then so be it. No dramas.

"We said no strings attached, but now we're in knots." – IG

It feels like something's wrong, out of place. Maybe we haven't formed that friendship yet. Maybe.

But maybe our beautiful spontaneity is what makes our fate. Maybe we need to veer off course to fall in love and be who we are. People come and go, who knows when you'll meet again, if ever you will. Why waste this moment on maybes?

"Romance has a life of its own. We're just passengers on a nonstop luxury cruise. We never thought it would be like this, and we don't want it to end." – IG

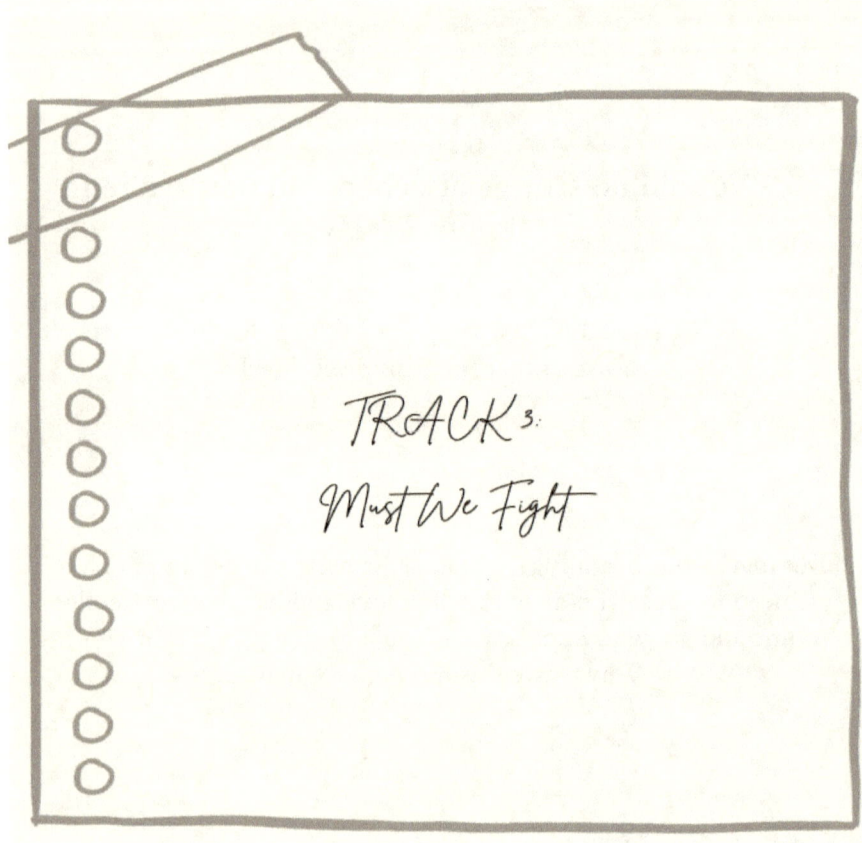

Playlist Companion

Paalam, Patawad by Moira Dela Torre

Stay by Lisa Loeb

Was This Love by Ben & Ben

Tuyo Na'ng Damdamin by Apo Hiking Society

Say Something by A Great Big World

Di Lang Ikaw by Juris

One More Try by Kuh Ledesma

Nakapagtataka by Rachel Alejandro

Anong Nangyari sa Ating Dalawa by Aiza Seguerra

Hanggang Dito Na Lang by TJ Monterde

"Love is no part of the dream world. Love belongs to Desire, and Desire is always cruel."

You told me you loved me
So, I really don't understand
How you could go behind my back
And be someone else's man

You said you'd be mine forever
But I have heard this one before
You told me not to be jealous
She was a friend, nothing more

You meant the world to me
And I trusted you with my heart
But now I have opened my eyes and see
It's time for us to part

"It may be resolved, but closure is a different thing."

Resolved: You know what the problem is, you've defined what has to be done, you do it, case closed.

This word is something that you're not so sure of
Sometimes you mean it
More often you don't
I say it frequently and think it's easy
For sometimes I mean it
More often I don't
I've said this you a million times
I say I mean it
Most likely I don't
Now that we're apart and said it to you
I want to take it back
I don't need goodbyes from you
Now I feel sorry for saying goodbye
I don't want to mean it
I don't want to lose you

"Someone's effort is a reflection of their interest in you."

The moment you think of love as a task that needs to be accomplished and requires painful effort on your part, and start waiting for appreciation because you don't feel it, is it still love?

The world you're in doesn't know who you are. When they see the guy, they think of another girl. The one he was with first before you ruined a relationship. So you had to claim your place and introduce yourself to the world by posting your pictures with him. Hoping that people will forget her, and start recognizing you. Lo and behold, you even had to control his account so that it shows you. Such a pity when you have to dictate. And hurting when you see looks that say you shouldn't be with him. It should be someone else. He should still be with her.

"Ipinaglaban Ka Ba? Minsan hindi ok pag 'mahal' ka. Kailangan kang pakawalan." - IG

Open to interpretation, given the last life changing events I had. True, right? Pero mas naniniwala ako na pag mahal, it's worth the fight.

"Cool Off - 2 words when side by side gives a meaning that's 2 words as well, and just as savage."

"Do we even have the tools to make it right the first time?"

In everything that we do, we should always have the right mindset, the heart, and the effort.

Projects based on the only skills and materials you have may get just an average or low grade.

Relationships based on initial feelings alone may fail or end.

"I Choose..."

He would say he loves me... Nothing has changed. Whatever we had, we still have. And I have to agree that we didn't change towards each other.

"Record Player"

"Love is the most vulnerable thing one will ever have, and you must learn to hold on to it loosely. So when it leaves, it won't exit as painfully."

Heard this in one of the open mic auditions of AGT from way back. I can't help but wonder, how does one hold on loosely? How do you hold back from something beautiful? How do you get to have that pause or stop button when you feel that every part, a hundred percent of you is giving in?

Love is a beautiful wonderful feeling. Something that one should not take lightly, and should be taken seriously. I guess the problem is, at least with me, is that I fall too fast and feel too deep. I succumb completely to all the beautiful gestures that one can only imagine happening in dreams, that I forget the importance of giving ourselves time.

Time to wait and get to know each other. Time to sort our feelings. Time to differentiate bliss from true love. Time to see that love also has its dark side. Time to ask the question "Is this really love". Time to prove that it is.

If only I have those record player buttons, I'd rewind to when things were simple between us…To that time when I haven't completely surrendered to your words and deeds. Then, I'd give ourselves time. Time to enjoy what we have when it was all rainbows and butterflies, no disappointments. Then I'd pause to enjoy the view, that wonderful feeling when we can't wait to just spend time with each other and have fun without expectations. And when the time is right, move forward in the same direction with certainty that we are doing the right thing.

I'm at the point of holding on too tightly to something that you're probably unsure of, and it will definitely hurt massively when it exits, no matter how short the time invested in it. I wish we had more time…Right now I'm feeling the opposite, and it's bothering me. Maybe I'm overthinking. I hope I am.

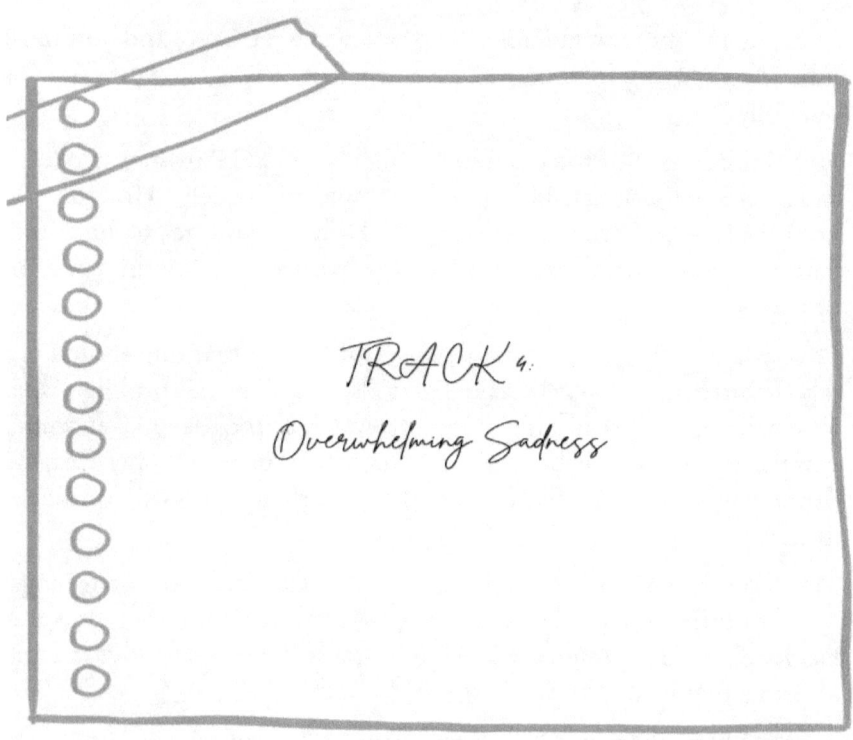

Playlist Companion

Sa Susunod na Habang Buhay by Ben & Ben

One Last Cry by Brian McKnight

The Best You Had by Nina Nesbitt

Kathang Isip by by Ben & Ben

Masyado Pang Maaga by Ben & Ben

Malaya by Moira Dela Torre

Can't Cry Hard Enough by Williams Brothers

All By Myself by Celine Dion

Love Me For What I Am by Karen Carpenter

Dadalhin by Regine Velasquez

SENSITIVE

Sensitivity is a relative term. What you may perceive as insensitive, may be not be the same with others.

This is where our hearts and minds step in.

We have to feel and think, and be sensitive to the people around us, to the feelings of others, to the hearts that might break if we do something wrong.

"Bakit kung sino pa ang nanloko, siya pa ang masaya ngayon?"

Our own version of happiness will come, in the cleanest and most opportune time.

When the time is right, you'd be surprised at how the universe can conspire to bring 2 souls together.

"There are wounds not visible on the body…that hurt way more than anything that bleeds."

SUNRISE

Painful times with silent tears
Hidden anger that no one hears
Will this unhappiness ever end?
Will no one spare a hand to lend?
Down and sad, I lose hope
Til I found my way to cope
I found a way to end my sighs
I found my hope in the new sunrise.

I MET YOU

Through the night
That gives glimmering light
You held me
You held me in your arms
We danced with the sweet music
And cold breeze that touched my skin
The stars shining bright seem to tell us
This would be forever
As I reached out for you
I felt nobody by my side
I opened my eyes
And found myself alone in the dark
Did you leave me?
Suddenly I realized
It was only in my dreams you held me
You danced with me
You loved me
Only in my dreams
I met you.

"The heart does not grow back."

We hope it does. But it doesn't.

Be careful to whom you give your heart to.

You only have one.

Once given to the wrong person, it will be returned broken.

But, someday, someone else's tight hugs can put the pieces back together.

"It's incredibly frustrating to forget, it must be an entirely other thing to be forgotten." – The Marble Collector, Cecelia Ahern

Such a pain to remember…
Even more painful to know you're forgotten.
Please remember me, never forget.
We were part of each other,
As fleeting as it may seem.
Never forget, please.
We were happy once.
They're all worth remembering,
Even the pain.

"Parting is such sweet sorrow..." - Shakespeare

There's this undeniable sadness felt when someone you've gotten used to leaves, when weekly routines are stopped, when the physical presence is just not there.

Presence though can be felt in different ways. Especially now with social media, no one is ever really apart from anyone across the globe.

All it takes is that strength between two people to be "together", and that faith that this will work. Use the time apart to grow stronger and miss each other. Use the loneliness to feel the importance of that person you love, and the impact he's brought in your life.

To my heart, you will miss him. Terribly. But he will be back soon. So cheer up princess, or the crown slips.

"Hayaan lang natin bumuhos ulan. Titigil din yan. Lalabas din araw mamaya. Tuloy ang field trip!"

The rain makes me nostalgic. Makes me emotional. It's bothering, but it's best to just let it be.

This feeling will pass.

Just like the sun who's trying it's best to shine through those dark clouds, happiness will persist. Happiness will win.

CRY LIKE THE REST

Where do you go when you disappear?
Where do you hide when you shed a tear?
On whom or what do you depend?
How much longer are you going to pretend?
I admire how you are so brave and strong
But I think that being closed up is wrong
You don't try to believe
You don't try to doubt
Because you've never known
What love is about
You try to have courage, faith and good will
But I think inside, you are vulnerable still
Keep it up, keep it strong
And do your best
Yet sometimes it help, come over
And cry like the rest.

MINE

In your smile
I see beyond your soul
So much guilt
So much sorrow

Your smile
A mirror of who you are
I look into your eyes
And I just know

Such sadness in your smile
So fragile, so alone
Then I realize
That smile is of my own.

"Let's say it's over...do you think after not seeing each other for months or years she'll still remember the love?"

Hmm. I guess it really depends on the people involved, how deep the love was, or the reason why it's over. A lot of factors really.

I then wonder, if you love someone so much and suddenly it's over, where does the love go? Maybe it will always be there. Maybe it will be forgotten. We decide whether it remains or we forget.

I guess the most that we can do as individuals who have loved and lost, is to keep the happy memories, and forget the ones that brought pain. It's okay to remember the love that was once there, but remember too that there is a reason why it didn't work out the first time.

If you believe in second chances, great. Just make sure that you make it right the second time around.

"Pag inaalala ko di ko pa rin gets why it had to happen. May purpose ba?"

Everything happens for a reason -- that's what people say when they run out of logical explanations as to why unexpected and hurtful things happen, when answering the question Why becomes difficult.

I guess we just have to trust the process. You may not understand or find meaning now why you have to go through it, but you will get through it. It is important to know the reasons why, but it is more important not to dwell so that you can surpass it.

TEARS

A sign of sadness
An indication of pain
Symbols of sorrow
That fall like rain

Each drop of water
Each single tear
Signifies aches
And reveals inner fears

YESTERDAY

Wasn't it yesterday
We met and fell in love
wasn't it yesterday
we felt we were up above
wasn't it yesterday
you said you'll be right here
wasn't it yesterday
your love for me was so dear
wasn't it yesterday
you kissed me so sweetly
wasn't it yesterday
you hugged me so tightly
wasn't it yesterday
we had the time of our lives
wasn't it yesterday
our love wasn't deprived
wasn't it yesterday
we never felt blue
wasn't it yesterday
you whispered I love you

They say that when you have a dream about something, it won't come true, and the opposite is what's going to happen.

But some also say that you dream about something because these are suppressed emotions and thoughts that manifest in our subconscious because we want them to come true so bad. As Cinderella said, "A dream is a wish your heart makes when you're fast asleep."

With the nightmare I had, I'd like to believe on the first one.

If dreaming is our doing since it is derived from our thoughts, then it means that interpreting it after it shakes us would also depend on us. In this real world, we are in control.

In reality, what we want so badly to happen requires persistence, that hunger to make it come true. But remember, if in dreams there are situations we don't like, all the more in reality.

It's comforting to know that you will wake up from nightmares. In real life, you can't really wake up from the bad things, but you can definitely act on it, to either prevent more horrible things from happening, or to get to where you want to be. For real.

"Ayoko na nga marinig, naririnig ko pa rin."

There are times when we just want to shut everything out and just be silent. When we don't want to hear anything about something or someone just so we can have some peace of mind. When we'd rather be deaf from all the things that may just be additional stress.

Sometimes, we can't help but hear even if we don't want to listen. Especially when it is our own inner voices that speak louder than reason. When these moments happen, may we learn to filter. Less stress and over thinking, more happy thoughts.

NEVER

Never whisper the words of love
If the feelings are not there
Never say I love you
If you don't really care
Never share your feelings
If you mean to break a heart
Never say you're going to
If you have no intentions to start
Never look into my eyes
If all you do is lie
Never say hello
If you really mean goodbye.

ALL ALONE

All alone
With the music in my head
Trying to recall special moments with you
Watching the sun set before my eyes
Wishing you're with me
Beside me all the time
But how can that be?
How can I be with you when you left me?
You left me with nothing
Nothing to ease the pain that I feel
You made it hard for me to love again
You took my heart with you
That's why I'm here
All alone
Wishing too hard you'd come back to me.

> "Natapos ko na rin ngayon ang isang libong paper cranes, at idinasal ko na sana bukas makakita ka na, agad agad.." – Kita Kita

I want to start making a thousand paper cranes. They say that once complete, your major wish will come true. Paniniwalaan ko na yata lahat…bumalik ka lang.

I want to be numb if I could.

Stop the heartache.

I'm already broken.

Breathe in, breathe out.

Please rest, my mind.

My heart, calm down.

Rest.

Ever had those time wherein you just feel like your entire system is down? When you just feel really emotionally drained that it takes a toll on your body?

Headache can be cured by pain relievers and rest, but the pains of a shattered heart is difficult to recover from.

Difficult, but not impossible. As my friend said, we always have a choice. Even not choosing is a choice.

Convo with an officemate...

R: Ano ba sinasabi nyang ginawa mo na di ka mapatawad?

O: Binalik ko siya sa nanay nya.

R: Ha? Bakit?

O: Kasi magugutom siya sa kin. Walang wala ako. Hindi ko na siya mabigyan ng magandang buhay.

R: So dahil dun ayawan na? Nasaan ang "in sickness and in health, for richer or for poorer?"

Sorry...I can't wrap my head around this reason. Isn't it that when you love someone, you stick with each other no matter what happens? Konting hindi makaranasan ng ginhawa, ayawan na? Abandonment na? This just doesn't sound right to me.

In The Greatest Showman, Barnum told his wife "This is not the life I promised you." And what did she say in return? "But I have all I ever need." Yan. Ganyan dapat. Hindi yung kung kelan ka kailangan dahil mahirap ang buhay, lalo mong tinalikuran, e kontento naman pala siya.

Consider your partner's views as well. If there are difficulties in reaching the dreams both of you built, always bear in mind these lines from the movie's song "A Million Dreams":

"However big however small,

Let me be part of it all,

Share your dreams with me.

You may be right,

You may be wrong,

Just say that you'll bring me along

To the world you see,

To the world I close my eyes to see..."

WHY

Why do I end up feeling guilty for what I've done?
Why do I feel lonely now that you're gone?
Why do I wish it never happened for it hurts both you and me?
Why do I call your name and wish you're beside me?
Why did I expect that you'd be with me forever?
Why did I think that when I know you'll love another?
Why do I feel hurt now that we're apart?
Why do I always pretend that it doesn't break my heart?
Why do I still want and need you as a friend?
Why only now do I look for the love you once sent?
Why do I long for your friendship now that you left me?
Now I feel really guilty for you're never coming back to me.

B: I wonder, if I await desperately in prayer, will I be able to meet someone I miss?

G: You do it to live. If you give up on waiting, the pain of loss will kill you. That's why you wait.

Heard this again. Got me thinking about you for the nth time. Amidst all these chaos, I am worried that something bad has happened to you.

Or is it the opposite? I know it's bad to think ill of anyone...but honestly, it has crossed my mind that something bad happened to you so that all these silences will have meaning. But then again, there is a reason: You have become a puppet of someone's doing. It is not of you to have grown so cold overnight, I'm sure of that.

Someone made you act that way. The "why" is clear, but the "how could you" is unanswered...Or both questions have the same answer that I just refuse to believe in.

"Eternal Sunshine of a Spotless Mind"

From one of the best movies I've seen: Eternal Sunshine of a Spotless Mind:

"I wonder...if the things that remind me of you, remind you of me."

Don't you just wish sometimes that you can just forget? Forget a place, a thing, an event, a date, a person.

But no. We are blessed with memory banks that just take everything in, good or bad. The memory has a mind of its own.

It persists. No matter how much you want to forget.

"Blank Space"

"I love the chaos and you love the game..." - Blank Space

Bakit nga ba? Alam ng magulo, sige pa rin. Alam ng masakit, go pa rin. Alam ng talo, laban pa rin. Pagmamahal pa ba, o dahil lang di matanggap na may mga bagay na nagtatapos? Pagiging martir pa ba, o dahil lang may galit at gusto ring makapanakit?

The chaos. It excites. It brings color in stories full of twists and turns. But ultimately... It hurts.

"Bagyo"

"Di ba nga, kung kelan paalis na, saka lumalakas...saka nakakapaminsala...parang yung dati mo." – officemate

"Naging Masaya"

"Let me get this straight: You cheated. She moved on with a guy and is actually happy. Now you're miserable and you think it's her fault? WILD MO PARE. Before you talk about your "pain", I hope you realize how much cheating hurts and how much it can mess someone up for good."

Yes, cheating hurts. Big time. Yes, it can mess you up. Big time too. But not for good. If that new someone comes along at the right time for the right reasons, he/she will make sure you forget about the pains of the past and give you what you deserve.

Painful memories will visit once in a while. Masakit kasi naging masaya. So dun na lang sa masaya tumingin. Half full, not half empty.

"2 Words"

Moments like this, on this so-called love month, I can't help but reminisce. Buti sana kung maganda ang mga naaalala. Eh hindi..

I am still traumatized by last year's scenario: Status changed from In a Relationship to Single on V-Day. Pero hindi naghiwalay o nag-away ha. Na-hack lang daw ang fb nya. Huwaw. Hindi ko naisip na prequel na pala to.

The following month after bitter confrontations...

"I'm sorry. 2 words. Yung 3 years namin nagawa nyang tapusin in 2 words."

Pero lahat naman nakakarecover. In my case, I've forgiven but will never forget. Sana nga nagalit na lang ako para mas madali.

Happy hearts day sa lahat ng pusong nagmahal, nasaktan, nagmahal at magmamahal muli.

From the movie #ValentinesDay

G: It has been a long time ago... I just wanted to tell you the truth.

B: The truth? Well, unfortunately, the truth makes everything else seem like a lie.

We were watching together. Forgetting the world for a while. Making each other feel as though nothing really changed. But then the title of the movie (and that specific part) brought back so much painful memories.

Suddenly someone so close felt so far away. Suddenly it felt like I was next to a stranger. Was there ever any truth in anything you said/say? I wouldn't want to know though if there are truths I need to know about coz that will just make everything else a lie.

"One of the hardest things you will ever have to do is to grieve the loss of a person who is still alive."

"If the past year were offered me again,
And choice of good and ill before me set,
Would I accept the pleasure with the pain,
Or dare to wish that we had never met?"

"Healing"

Sabi ng priest sa healing mass kanina, "Hawakan mo kung anong masakit sayo at papagalingin ka Niya. Sabihin mo gagaling ako. Sabihin mo magaling na ako.."

Sorry na. Dun talaga ko napahawak e. Wish it were that easy to heal, right? Yung tipong trust and faith lang ok na. Yung i-pray over ka lang healed na.

I guess trust and faith is 50%, and the other half is the willingness to be healed.

Healing a shattered heart doesn't need a miracle, and I've seen miracles happen. So it's definitely not impossible. It just takes time.

"Hello...Goodbye"

I want to be someone's favorite hello and hardest goodbye.

This is just the best feeling ever, right? Ang hirap lang mahanap. Most of the time there are favorite hellos...but easy goodbyes.

"Dark Past"

G1: Haay ginawa talaga nyang dark ang past ko

G2: Mas mabuti ng dark past with bright future 'no. Kaysa naman the other way around. Enough na. Past na nga e.

Some things end, while some are meant to last forever. Some memories we think of, we feel good about them, and wish that we have collected more. And there are some that would make us feel bad inside after reminiscing. We end up thinking who are they making memories with now?

If memories start giving you that stab in your heart, that moment when your chest tightens and you just have to breathe deeply to release the stress, are they still worth pondering on? Bad vibes yan!

Better to just leave it in your dark past and look forward to a brighter future. A future where you can create more memories that will just leave you smiling and craving for more.

Cheers to a brighter future with people who are as excited as you to create happy memories with!

"Basha"

Bilang uso si Bea this month...

Totoo naman di ba? There is that hope at the back of our heads sometimes, na sana tayo na lang, tayo pa rin, tayo na lang ulit, ang nasa lugar ng bago nya. Lalo na pag nakikita mo silang masaya. Bakit? Because that happiness used to be yours. Kaya masakit, kaya gustong maibalik, kasi naging sobrang saya.

I'd like to believe that every time I feel the Basha in me, na hindi specific person ang namimiss ko. That I just miss the feeling of being loved, calling someone mine, having that ecstatic happiness you turn to when your day gets tough.

There's a Basha in all of us. The one in me...well she's annoying and hoping. Why not? E nandyan si Popoy who's feeding the hope.

"The Source"

It's both a good and a bad thing to realize that the person you once thought to be your source of happiness, is slowly becoming your source of pain. Good because you're moving forward, bad because you don't want this to happen.

"Cry"

"Cry with someone. It's more healing than crying alone."

There is nothing more comforting than crying your heart out with people who genuinely care.

So keep your truest and most honest besties at bay. I can guarantee they will do the following:

Let you cry until you're embarrassed and look like a turtle with puffy eyes.

Let you drink wine even if you don't drink at all.

Sing heartbreak and moving on songs even if you don't sing.

Be your brain and your senses when all that's working in your body is your heart and tear ducts.

Tells you honestly when it's enough.

Then later on you'll realize that all is well in the world again. If sadness creeps in again, repeat! The besties would be brave enough as well to tell you, "OA ka na. Sige tuloy mo lang yan. Hindi ka naman nakikinig so wala na kaming magagawa, pero nandito lang kami."

"There are a few things sadder in this life than watching someone walk away after they've left you, watching the distance between your bodies expand until there's nothing…but empty space and silence."

"I heard a song, and it made me think of you. The song ended, and it made me think of you too."

"Iniwan sa Ere"

From a heartfelt phone call...

"Hindi man lang nya naisip na maiiwanan nya ko mag-isa sa decision na ginawa nya?"

Uncontrollable circumstance: the way people think and act. Madalas nasasaktan na lang tayo dahil sa mga desisyon at kilos ng iba dahil we overthink. We then influence our thoughts and feelings towards the situation that we have no control over.

My dear, sinabihan ka pa rin naman pagkatapos nakapagdesisyon. That still serves as something. Eh di sana hindi na lang nya nabanggit at all.

The problem with people is that "issue" is a relative term. Pwedeng it means the world to you, but not for the other. We cannot dictate how people will react to something. All we can do is appeal to their sensitive side by means of being honest, but still, we can't dictate how they should react.

You feel bad because of failed expectations. So I guess the best that you can do is don't expect na lang. Kapag may nangyaring maganda in the coming days, no matter how little, naku, para kang nanalo sa lotto nyan dahil hindi mo inexpect.

"You closed our chapter the way it had begun; all of a sudden, all at once…"

"Obliviate"

Watching #DeathlyHollows...

Sana totoo yung isang flick and swish lang ng wand mo ma-wipe out ka na sa memory ko. Yung parang walang nangyari, wala akong nakilalang ikaw, wala akong naramdamang sakit.

Or better yet, sana ako na lang may magic tapos buburahin ko lahat ng memories mo of her. Palagay ko mas bet ko to!

Pero shempre... Back to reality. Walang ganyan. We all have to go through pain and recovering from it when we lose someone. Pray na lang talaga.

"Hyperthymesia"

"It is the rare ability to recall nearly all past experiences in great detail. The causes of HSAM (highly superior autobiographical memory) are currently unknown, but some theories suggest that it may have biological, genetic, or psychological origins. There is currently no way to diagnose hyperthymesia formally."

Oh I don't like this. Not one bit.

"Gaya ng Dati"

Chat convo with cousins since I was mega-ranting about commute frustrations...

Me: Ayoko na magbus! Lintik na yan! 5hrs to get home?! Unacceptable. Babalik na lang ako sa dati kong route and transpo. May hassles pa rin pero lesser evil.

Minsan, babalik at babalik tayo sa dati, not because it's better by much, but because it's more convenient in some ways. There are things that we're used to that we'd rather stick with than try new ones kahit masakit rin sa ulo. Minsan kasi no choice naman. So ang ending, balik sa nakasanayan.

Narelate ko na naman sa buhay... Kahit masakit ka sa ulo, babalik at babalik ako sayo. Hindi lang dahil ikaw ang nakasanayan ko, kundi dahil mas panatag ako sayo kumpara sa kung sinu-sino.

"Settling"

Pinag-iisip pa rin si ate ng mga mahaderang friends...

"What are this guy's merits? Meron ba? Or did you cling to him to have someone around?"

After bitter separations caused by 3rd parties, more often than not, walang naiiwang mag-isa. But it doesn't necessarily mean both are in their ideal relationships. Kadalasan, para lang hindi maiwang nag-iisa. "Kung meron ka, meron din ako" attitude. At pag ito ang pinairal, malamang hindi na pinag-isipan kung may merits ba ang new partner. Basta lang may bago ka rin.

Girls, know what you want in a person. What you can and cannot compromise. Gawa ng checklist. If there are non-negotiable traits that you see in the other, why waste time and effort.

And the most important: Wag ipilit para lang masabing hindi ka mag-isa. Bad yan.

Sometimes the only reason why you won't let go of what makes you sad is because it was the only thing that made you happy.

Mother and son convo...

S: He doesn't reply (showing me a text message he sent to his dad weeks ago). See. Why?

M: Maybe he changed numbers. Or maybe he's dead, I dont know.

S: Look at this game mommy (changes the topic)

M: Hey, I just told you that your dad may be dead and you don't care?

S: I care about you more.

I was caught off guard. I don't know what he means and couldn't construct a proper question. I had no response. This little man has clearly stopped caring earlier than I did. Or did he?

If there's one thing (among many) I've learned from this quarantine period, it's that you'll know who matters and who don't. Alongside with it though, you'll also know who really cared and didn't, because you were just...forgotten.

"You will never know the value of a moment until it becomes a memory."

"Love doesn't grow well, fed on pain."

"Walking on eggshells"

That's how it is with you. It seems like one wrong text and all the happiness and love from days past are all gone. I know that we don't need each other. Our lives are complete without each other's existence. Sabi mo nga, palamuti at pampalasa lang dapat tayo sa isa't isa. Pero ang hirap paniwalaan nito, at least on my end, when there's this nagging pain in my chest in wanting to at least hear from you and tell me that everything is alright, that it was just a small spat we had earlier.

Mahirap ang chill or to be relaxed about this, when one's mindset is that I am not needed, but just wanted. Not sure if the message of the video is easy to live by. It's hard to live with the shadow of pain and abandonment looming around.

"Sometimes we don't want to heal because the pain is the last link to what we've lost."

"Every loss leaves a hole in your heart. El Maestro, as you may have surmised, suffered a great loss earlier in his life, one that led him to a drunkard's despair. His wife died. The beautiful woman who would lead him from the stage and plant a kiss on his lips. Once she was gone, he wanted nothing from this earth. He let himself sink—into melancholy, into drinking, into a haunted, restless sleep. If he could have unplugged his heart and shut the lights on his memory, he would have."

"Humans grow dizzy from new affection."

This is exactly how I felt during the first few months and then gone now. Just like that.

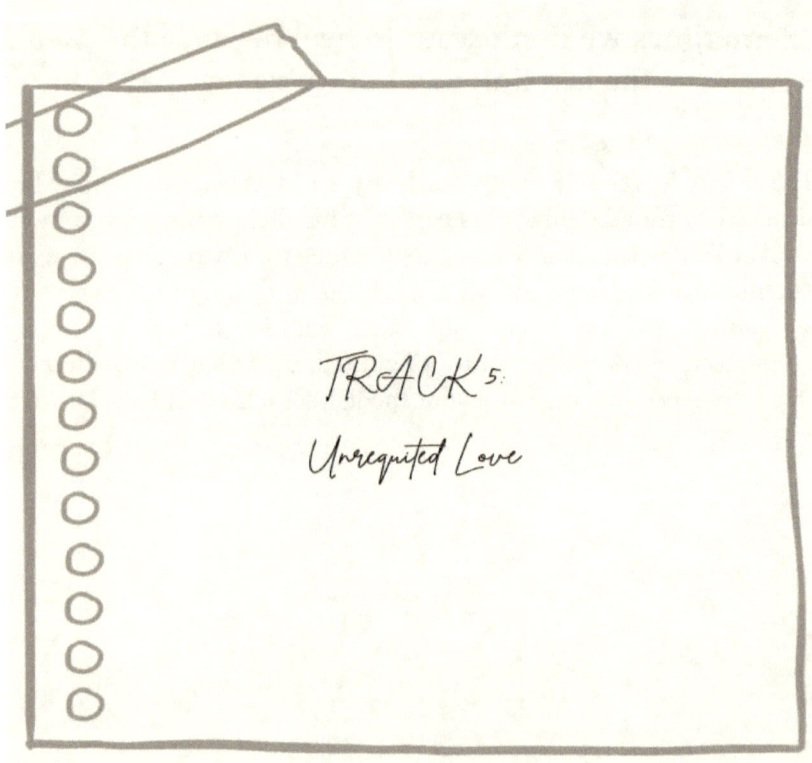

Playlist Companion

Akin Ka Na Lang by Morisette Amon

Kung Di Rin Lang Ikaw by December Avenue

I'll Have To Say I Love You In A Song by Jim Croce

Gravity by Sara Bareilles

Pagdating ng Panahon by Aiza Seguerra

If The World Was Ending by JP Saxe and Julia Michaels

Love Don't Let Me Go by Angelina Jordan

Kay Tagal by Rachel Alejandro

Why Can't It Be by Kaye Cal

Rewrite The Stars by Anne-Marie and James Arthur

WAITING

#overheard from passengers waiting for shuttle service:

"I've been waiting forever... Feels like I'm waiting for nothing..."

Waiting in vain. The waiting game is never fun. It will make you think of letting go and giving up. Or, it can make you hope as well that once what you're waiting for is presented to you by the universe, that it will be worth the wait.

I guess what's important is making sure that expectations are set that someone is waiting when told to wait.

"Pag kasama ko siya nakikita ko naman na mahal niya ko e...Pero hindi ko maintindihan bakit hindi ako?" - Bridgette, Camp Sawi

Convo with son on video game...

A: I hate this!!! (Frustrated that tablet restarted)

M: What's wrong?

A: It does this every time! Pag restart when I turn on my worlds are gone!

M: 'Nak, if a game already starts to be frustrating and gives you that negative feeling, then it's no longer a game. Games are suppose to be fun. So delete it. Just play a different game. One that you can save.

A: But I want this.

M: Sabi ko nga e. E di push. Wag ko lang marinig ulit na galit ka na naman.

Games. We play them too, even at 40. Maybe even when we're 60 or 90. Ang hindi lang maganda is minsan tao, isip at puso na ang pinaglalaruan. Masaya kadalasan kasi laro nga. Pero kung masakit na, laro pa ba? If you can accept the idea of things restarting after something bad has happened, then go. Laro pa more. Naaayos naman pala e.

Ultimately, I'd say do what makes you happy. Deadma na sa minsang sakit, basta nagagawan ng paraan. It will not always be rainbows and butterflies in games.

#overheard from a lover's quarrel:

"You made me wait. Ano ba talaga ko sa buhay mo?!?"

Girls talk too much when in pain. And too loud actually. A lot more was said but I'll give her privacy.

I feel you.

Relationships have to be labeled. Otherwise, what is it? Labels serve as security. If someone asks you if he's your boyfriend, how do you respond? If he suddenly ends up with someone, do you have the right to complain or feel bad? No. Because technically, there is no clarity. There is no "me and you". There is no "us". You are alone in your voyage through dark stormy seas that will never find its calm.

Are you going to settle for not having someone to call your own? You go, girl! Good job in being strong enough to ask. Some would just remain quiet for fear of getting answers they don't want to hear.

Know your worth. Keep your values. Maintain self-respect. Someone far better will come along and will make you feel that you don't need to ask those stupid questions.

"Matutuwa ba ako na friends kami, or malulungkot ako dahil naging ganun na lang?"

Define Friends.

Bargaining. The 3rd "stage" of bereavement according to Kubler-Ross, for any kind of loss that's experienced.

We all go through this when someone leaves unexpectedly.

Consciously or not. We will always bargain for something to be saved so that remembering the good memories will not be as painful. We tell ourselves that it would be better to have something than nothing at all. After all, we were happy.

I can only speak for what I believe in -- I am a believer that if something can be saved, save it. No matter how little or different from the way it used to be, as long as it's clear and you can take the blows of the shift in status, then why not.

On the other hand, a part of me also believes that if past lovers become friends, it means that they still love each other, or it was never that kind of love to begin with.

"Agawan Blues"

Lots of life lessons earlier during training. Why? Coz it's about Acquisitions and Moves. In short, marami na namang nakarelate sa mga issue ng AGAWAN at PAGMAMAY-ARI.

Here are a few life lessons from overheards:

- Ang dami mo ng sinayang na oras, hindi naman pala sayo.

- Pag pupunta na sa kabila, hindi kailangang magpaalam sa current. Magugulat na lang si current na may bago na pala.

- Pag lumipat na or natunugan mong may iba ng napupusuan, try to retain. Give your best offers.

- Habang nasa iyo pa, kahit may bad record, tanggapin mo pa rin. Patawarin mo. Baka naman nagbago na.

- Pag nagpunta na sa iba tapos babalik sayo pagkatapos ng bad record duon sa kabila, pwede mo ng tanggihan. Baka gawin ulit sayo e.

- Pag walang may ari, kunin mo na! Arte pa? Maunahan ka pa ng iba.

Talaga nga naman. There's a lot to learn in class.

"Sometimes the bad people don't know that what they're doing is bad."

I guess this is true for those who only think of themselves. Initially when we are about to do something, we ask ourselves pertinent questions like is this going to be beneficial to me, am I not hurting anyone by doing this, is it going to do more good than bad?

With these "bad" people, they just stop at the first question.

As mature individuals, we should know how to weigh things and be sensitive to what others may feel before we decide.

It won't hurt to pause, think, and do good.

"He knows how to keep her on a leash. And she lets him."

"Forgotten. Not."

"I've never forgotten him. Dare I say I miss him? I do. I miss him. I still see him in my dreams. They are nightmares mostly, but nightmares tinged with love. Such is the strangeness of the human heart. I still cannot understand how he could abandon me so unceremoniously, without any sort of goodbye, without looking back even once. The pain is like an axe that chops my heart." - Life of Pi (man to tiger friend)

Nangyayari sa totoong buhay, at sa tao, ang mga eksenang ganito.

"Abandon unceremoniously"? - Nandyan kahapon na mahal na mahal ka, tapos limot ka na bukas. Animal lang. Ganon.

And the pain that's like an axe...It disappears but comes back all the time.

> "We have to allow our hearts to break a little sometimes so that someone else's would never have to break again."

This is the kind of love parents have for their children. Sacrifices are made for them and it's difficult to explain that there some things we do even if it breaks our hearts, just so they can be happy. Unconditional love, that's what is.

If only everyone realizes that this is the best kind of love. If only people see unconditional love in front of them and take care of it so that they don't lose it. If only. What a wonderful world it would be.

> "She was a giver. Always poured too much of love. Never realized watering a rock doesn't make it soft."

"Mothering"

I feel like a mother who needs to know his whereabouts. Not that I'm complaining. Hey, I love the attention. But, it has come down to just this. Around 1 to 2 messages in a day -- just to tell me he's on his way to work, and going home from work. Nothing in between. Very seldom sweet nothings.

Once I start getting his attention about it, he overreacts coz he hates drama.

So, I'll just let it be. Maybe I need to give him time to miss the attention too. For real.

"You call it hope -- that fire of fire! It is but agony of desire!" - Edgar Allan Poe

You HOPE to possess what your heart DESIRES.

Hoping can be positive since you see yourself striving and giving your all to get what you desire.

But it also gives you agony when you fail to get what you want...

"It's okay to fight for someone WHO loves you. It's not okay to fight for someone TO love you. There's a huge difference."

"Love is not hard. Being with the wrong person is."

"Placebo Effect"

"Just because this is the status quo, doesn't mean it's right." - convo with a friend

Status quo. To keep the things the way they presently are.

Some would subject themselves to what they have gotten used to in order to maintain what they think is right, what they think is love. Why? So as not to break the status quo. Masaya naman minsan e. Ok na rin. They have conditioned their thoughts that it's better to have the present set up, no matter how messy, just to keep something. Mabuti ng meron kaysa wala. Mas ok ng merong kung ano man, kahit hindi totoo. Placebo effect.

But is it worth all the pain, inconvenience and discomfort? No. If it has come to a point that there's no longer effort from both parties to make things better and there's only acceptance of the "sometimes pretty" status quo, then there's no point holding on to it. It's not right and just for both of you.

"I might deserve better, but it's you I want."

You lie. You cheat. You play.
But still I stay.
People like you should be left alone.
People like me should not settle.
But still I do.
I like. I miss. I love.
I'm just not ready to give up the game.
Not now. Maybe not ever.

"LOVE. It overpowers PAIN."

It's so easy for you to lie.
No rehearsals needed.
It's so easy for me to believe.
No convincing needed.
You're a buffet of lies.
And I'm very much hungry to dig in.

"Lies"

"Tanong sha ng tanong ayaw naman marinig sagot. Masakit daw yun marinig. Bakit nagtatanong pa?"

Bakit nga ba? Maybe it's not that people don't want to hear truths that hurt. Maybe they just want to hear pleasantries to sugarcoat the pain, and then be the one to interpret things the way their minds and hearts see fit.

Kung napapanahon na at kakayanin na ng puso ang katotohanan, sa oras na lang yun makikinig.

For now, maybe pleasantries and comforting lies are better. Baka hindi pa sha ready na tanggapin na lang lahat ng masakit na katotohanan. Kung sino man sha.

"In the end, we all just need someone who would choose us. Over everyone else, under any circumstances."

Still you.
Always you.
At the end of every damn day.

"What's not important is not in your head. What's not in your heart doesn't come out of your mouth."

"It Has No Heart"

Minsan ang relasyon ganyan. May rhythm. May beat. May routine. Pero minsan nakasanayan lang, wala ng puso.

To distinguish though, is difficult. After many years... How do you know if it's still love or just the fear of losing something you've gotten used to?

"Yakap"

Moments like these make me believe your every lie, and forgive you all over again.

Until when will I be under your spell? What can break this?

But the ultimate question is, do I want to be free from you?

If you're in a relationship where you have to stay hidden, you're not suppose to be in it. Period.

"Cage"

"A bird in a cage still knows it's in a cage, even if the bars are made of gold."

I'm still at the point wherein I believe your every word. Crazy as it may sound, but when you say you love me, it still gives me that overwhelming feeling. It transports me to a world I've always wanted to be in -- where you love me, and I love you back, and there's no one getting in the way. I like that world. I look forward to those messages, and even ask for more. I helped create the cage I don't want to get out off.

Now I haven't heard from you in days. No messages. No phone calls. Nothing that will make this cage worth being trapped in. The silence is killing me. I can't breathe in this situation. I want to be free coz I'm alone here.

Ramdam na ramdam ko na kahit saan ko palang anggulo tingnan, nakakulong pa rin ako. Hindi makawala. Habang nasa labas ka at malaya.

I am not a piece by piece person. I want all of you… or nothing at all.

> "You haven't changed. You still talk too much...then none at all.."

Possible ba ang "Mahal ko kayo. Hindi na yan magbabago. Mahalaga ka sa kin." pero bigla namang nawalang parang bula? I don't think so.

I want these thoughts to be over quick, the same way that I fell too fast and felt too much.

I want to believe you, I guess that's why I held on for a very long time, but actions really speak louder than words. This silence deafens me, and is killing me over and over. Yes, pain demands to be felt, at damang dama ko na. Sobra. Tama na.

> "Hindi lahat ng tinatanim nabubuhay, kahit gaano pang panahon ang ibinuhos nyo dyan."
>
> #overheard from a plantita

> "Can you hear me? Can you taste my pain? For love has no other desire but to fulfill itself...And to deny yourself the pleasure of the pain is to love selfishly."

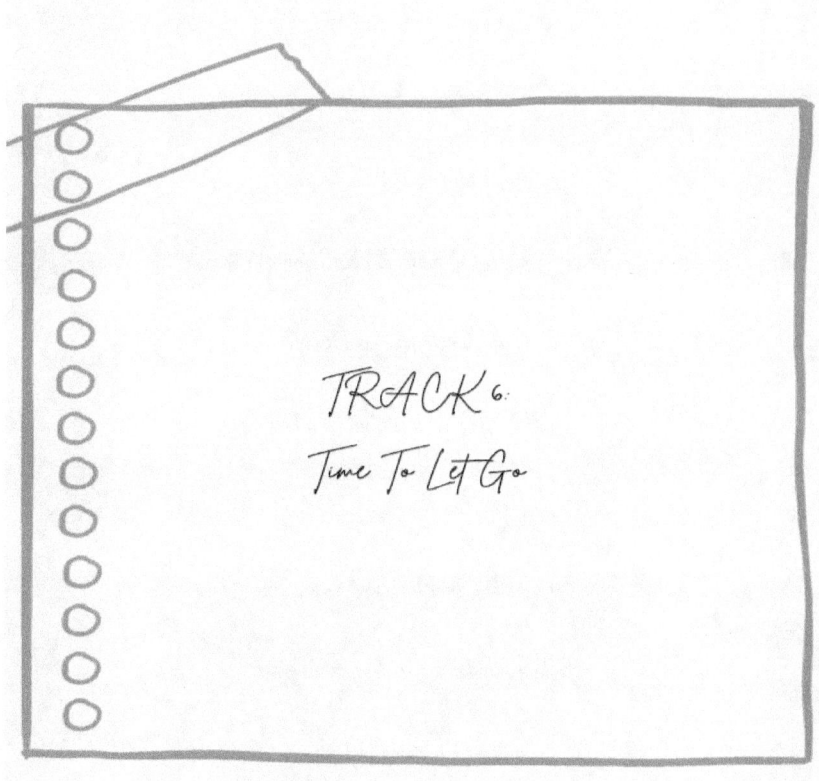

Playlist Companion

Leaves by Ben&Ben

Someday by Nina

Saglit by Moira Dela Torre

I'll Never Love This Way Again by Dionne Warwick

Maybe by Jensen and Reese

I Fall All Over Again by Dan Hill

Need You Now by Lady A

Oks Lang by John Roa

Huling Sandali by December Avenue

Paubaya by Moira Dela Torre

Like snowflakes and stardust,
We appear, we vanish.
We may inspire some,
But we are just passing through.

"Don't give it power by talking about it."

There are some things we do that we say mean nothing. We say it will no longer affect us. It is what it is. The situation will never change. It will forever be like this.

So why still think about it? Why dwell? If you constantly think about it, analyzing it to bits, then obviously, it matters. It is powerful enough to mess with your head, then it messes up your actions.

Old habits die hard.
Or live on forever.
Like warm cozy beds.
Easy to get in to, difficult to get out of.

"Graduation"

"Parang graduation lang yan. Feeling mo lahat sila mamimiss mo so you hug everyone as tight as you can and it's difficult to let go. But at the end of the day/ceremony, you forget about most of them and you move on with life."

It is challenging not to feel a bit of loneliness when you let go of people, things and events that you got used to. That's why as people with beating and feeling hearts, the tendency is to hold on to the past because we are scared of the future's uncertainty.

We can always cherish the past, but this should not hinder us from embracing the present, and look forward to the future.

It's not the future that scares us. It's the thought that the past was the best that makes us unsure of moving and letting go.

As the saying goes, "We don't know what the future holds." So have the courage to just take each day at a time, and make new memories as you go along.

"The most beautiful thing about love is that we always have a choice. The tragic thing though is we often forget we have brains."

Love is a choice, and what a beautiful choice it is to fall in love. Sometimes we even say that it just happened, we have no control over it. We gave in to what we were feeling at the moment and of course, want it to last forever.

But, the moment you already have to choose between staying in love or letting go, make sure you let your brain step in. The heart will always refuse to let go. It doesn't think. It will just go for what it feels even if it gets broken in the process. The brain would be the one to guide the heart in moments when it's blinded and consumed by emotions.

A convo between friends about the pimple scar I have that wouldn't go away no matter what I used on it.

F: Antagal na nyan. Mashado mo ng minahal. Dapat mabura na yan.

R: Antagal na nga e. Kahit ano gawin ko ayaw talaga mawala! Napamahal na sa balat ko. Gusto nandyan lang.

F: Mashado ng nasanay na nakadikit sayo.

R: Feeling ko forever na tong nandito.

In our lifetime, there will be experiences and even people who will stay with us even if we no longer want to. Some memories would just keep popping up in our heads no matter how hard we try to forget. Some would just continue to stay in our lives no matter what happens. Nasanay na kasi ang utak at katawan natin na nandyan sila.

Kung hindi na nakakabuti katulad ng pimple scar na nakakapanget lang, kailangan talaga mabura yan. Bottomline is, do what needs to be done so that it doesn't harm you anymore.

Kung kinakailangan na ng derma, punta na.

"Don't confuse a lesson for a soulmate."

What is a soulmate? A soulmate is someone who comes into your life unexpectedly. One that just has an instant connection with you, that requires no effort at all. We've had our share of people coming into our lives and thinking "he's the one." Then one day, it all ends. Your soulmate will never crush your heart and soul, will never shatter your dreams, and will never let you go. If he does, then he is just a lesson you have to learn from.

The challenge is learning how to keep the lessons and completely let go of the pain, the anger, and the happiness he brought.

"Make peace with your past so it won't screw up the present."

Past relationships may haunt us for the rest of our lives if there is no proper closure. As long as there's anger, we will never be at peace. When there is no peace, we will never be happy for the other. If there's always a bad feeling whenever you remember, then it ruins your disposition, which then affects the present, or even the future.

Don't let the ghost of the past linger. The only thing you should be pondering about from a past that didn't work out are the lessons you've learned. That is if you did learn anything from it.

"If you don't heal what hurt you, you'll bleed on people who didn't cut you."

If you're mad at one person, make sure you don't lash this out on the world. Sometimes I am guilty of being ill-tempered on people who have nothing to do with what or who is letting me down.

To those who are "victims" of my "walking out EQ" and start asking themselves why coz you didn't really do anything wrong, I'm sorry. It's not you, it's me.

"When things change inside you, things change around you."

Change. Strong word.

True isn't it? When you start changing how you feel about people and things, and like in general, your actions change too.

Sabi nga ng kumare ko, "Ang 1+1 laging 2 yan. You can't expect a different result. Gawin mo kayang 1+1×5? Yan for sure iba na sagot dyan."

Oo nga naman. Being a leader for so long, I should know better than to keep on doing the same things and expecting different results. Sa tagal ko na ring "broken", dapat alam ko ng walang magbabago.

Action planning to get to your desired goal is easy. Flawless execution and follow-through? Ayan na ang challenge.

The question is: Am I up for it?

From an article...

"How a male treats a woman is NOT a reflection of HER worth. Nor is it a reflection of anything she LACKS or is not doing. An overly macho, mentally weak, sensitive-minded male knows he does not DESERVE a strong-minded woman. In his mind, he thinks one day she will mentally awaken to the realization she deserves better than him & leave him. This is why males cheat on a woman, to have POWER over her. He cheats on her to boost his ego."

So for those who stick around after the cheating because of the thinking that he'll see you're more worthy than the other, think again.

"Lakas ng ulan! When it rains, it pours."

True in life as well. Months ago, I was overwhelmed by so many challenges financially and emotionally that I was on the brink of giving up. I was wounded, and broken, and can't stop asking why those things had to happen. Then I told myself, I would not be given anything I couldn't handle.

A few months later, I was blessed to have a rewarding job, a new environment that would get my mind off unpleasant memories, and someone who brought back my confidence and treated me the way I deserve to be treated (you know who you are).

When we're in those stormy moments, we just have to know how to handle the dark clouds, because the sun never really left.

"Spiderman"

"You have done this to me, again and again, Peter. I can't live with this anymore. I break up with you. I break up with you." - Gwen Stacey

"ATM"

"10 yrs kami nagsama nun. Never siya nareplace or nawala. Kahit sabi ng iba palitan ko na raw kasi pinahihirapan na ko minsan, di pa rin ako naglet go. Minsan nga ayaw na siya tanggapin, ipipilit ko pa rin -- konting himas ko lang and try again, gagana rin. E dumating na sa point na di na talaga pwede. Di na gumagana kahit anong pilit ko. Wala na talaga akong makukuha kahit pa ulit-ulitin kong ipagpilitan. Kailangan ko ng talagang palitan."

Saying goodbye to my 10yr old ATM card. Clingy pa naman ako.

"One day you'll realize that there are some people you'll never see again. At least not in the same way."

"Ghost In You"

"Parang multo lang...Minsan nagpaparamdam."

Sometimes we act like ghosts. We would bother others by making them feel us, even if we're dead to them. Ghosts do that because they need to be felt. They have unfinished businesses to fulfill.

In life, there would be times wherein we would feel like ghosts...As though people just pass by and we go unnoticed. There would be those who'd make us feel invisible.

But then, there would also be those who'd demand our presence too. Those who'd pray and beg for us to be there and give a little bit of attention. Those who will appreciate that we came to touch their lives.

Find that person (or people) who'd appreciate every minute with you while you're around. In return, be sensitive to those around you that you may unknowingly be treating like ghosts. Appreciate them too.

"Some Just Stay Broken"

"Some things just take time. Some things just stay broken."

Some say time heals all wounds. But this quote I heard says otherwise. I think I believe the latter.

Sometimes when we feel that we've moved on, something happens that makes us still feel a bit of pain. Maybe that reminds us that there are instances and people that really broke some part of us, no matter how much we deny it, and it hasn't really healed after time.

And maybe it won't be healed or whole again, but, it has made us stronger, and hopefully wiser.

"Let It Go"

"Learn to let go, and allow blessings to flow."

A lot of people are stuck in situations they can't control -- the past, failed expectations, other people's decisions. Refusing to move. Hoping that if they stand still, the world will stop with them, and the situation will be better all of a sudden. Thinking "Maybe if I don't do anything, things will be back to what they used to be."

There is a reason why relationships end. There is a reason why some things don't last. Whatever it is, it all boils down to the fact that it/he/she no longer fits your life.

It's time to let go as fast as you can, or you'll miss seeing and appreciating the blessings that pass you by. Be smart in figuring out when to hold on, or if it's time to break free.

"Why?"

"Maybe it's not about why they left. Maybe it's about why you stayed."

Not maybe. Surely. The question is Why. Ang tanong na di masagot sagot.

You will never really understand what's going on in someone else's mind. Moreso, control it. What is controllable though are your own thoughts, which then dictates your actions. So wag na isipin ano pa mga dahilan ng pagkawala o pag alis. Pag-isipan na lang kung bakit ka pa nandyan.

"Marie Kondo"

"Start discarding, all at once, intensely and completely. Keep only those things that speak to your heart."

For those decluttering today (or have been decluttering for the longest time)...

Kaya mo yan. Let go na of the kalat in your life.

"Identifying Needs"

Phone call scenario -- probe pa more kasi di mo alam concern e...Tapos hirap pa mag explain ang kausap. Mga 10 minutes na siguro lumipas, then you find out you need to transfer to another dept...

"Ang tagal ng oras na sinayang ko, hindi pala para sa kin."

Hmmm. Sakit nyan! Time is such a big investment. Kaya nga time breaks more hearts than love. Pag ang oras nasayang, no turning back. Si love, pwede pang dumating ulit.

Malay mo may magtransfer din sayo kasi hindi rin pala para sa kanya.

"End Game"

"Everybody wants a happy ending, right? But it doesn't always roll that way. Maybe this time. I'm hoping you play this back... it's in celebration. I hope families are reunited. I hope we get it back, in somewhat like a normal version of the planet has been restored if there ever was such a thing."

"For once, I want to love without thinking 'What if I lost him'?"

"True"

The conversation over the phone sounded real. Sounded sincere. Ang hirap talikuran. After many many months, that moment ko lang naramdaman na ang sorry niya totoo, that we have something undeniably real.

What we have was real..but not ideal. Naungkat ang mga pagkakamali, ang mga pagkukulang. Admittedly, they're all true. Surprisingly, we both felt it was useless to still argue about it.

"I may not always be around, but please know in your heart na mahal kita at mahalaga ka sa akin. Hindi na magbabago yan. I still want to see you and be with you as much as I can at alam mo yan."

Panghahawakan ko yan. Paniniwalaan ko yan. Sana kayanin kong tuluyan ng mamaalam.

"Heal"

They say time heals all wounds. Does it really? Or are we just learning to suppress our feelings of sadness because we have no choice? I know there is always a choice. In this case it's either I allow to subject myself to being a victim or be strong enough to shut everything out. My head tells me the right thing to do is value myself, but my heart refuses to let go.

I have tried several times -- blocking, no communication -- but it has done me more harm than good. Maybe its because of the inconsistency. Marupok e. Konting lambing, defenses down again.

I know for a fact that I am broken, and I'm hoping that time will really heal me. No one really knows, not even myself, how long this will take.

Sometimes it's difficult to move on from people and things that you've gotten used to. Sometimes, not because the relationship is over, everything ends with it. You've shared memories with that person. It may have ended badly, but there is a way to move on from the pain and ugly truth: Think of the happy beginning and the wonderful middle. It's all in how you'll control your thoughts.

"Do not get upset with people or situations. Both are powerless without your reaction."

"We became strangers....with memories."

Wounds heal but leave scars. We humans need a reminder for everything, even for lessons that we learn the hard way.

"Matatanggap mo pa ba ang taong nawalan ng reason to stay, pero nagkaroon ng reason to come back?"

Someday, we will forget the hurt, the reason we cried, and who caused us the pain.

We will finally realize that the secret of being free

is not revenge, but letting things unfold in their own way and own time.

After all, what matters is not the first but the last chapter of our life which shows how well we ran the race.

So smile, laugh, forgive, believe, and love all over again.

Love is staying, but staying doesn't always mean loving.

"Asawa"

In had this convo with the Titas I've been with since HS about love, marriage, and being lonely...

Tita1: Sinasabi nila try dating kse bata pa ko. Nung nakaramdam ako ng feeling na appreciated ka parang ang sarap pala. Ibang happiness naman. Naisip ko if last year ko ginawa di ko maappreciate since ayoko talaga last year pero now identified ko na may kulang sa buhay ko or gusto ko na ulit to have a partner. Im not going to get married again gusto ko lang at the end of the day meron mag pat on my back and tell me ok lang lahat...whenever i feel lost gusto ko lang yung may hahawak ng kamay ko.

Tita2: Nalungkot ako sa sabi mo for some reason. I've never been married. Lahat kayo naexperience na ninyo yan. I've been alone longer. Still am.

Tita3: Lahat tyo may kanya kanyang journey. Hindi naman porket naging married kami mas nakalamang kami syo. You had your share of partners too. Baka nga mas naging wife ka pa at some point kesa dun sa mga talagang wife. Being Married may be just a title, nasa puso yan and sa pinagsamahan nyo.

Maraming food for thought. Awakenings. And this all started when one was asking if it's ok to date again. When we said of course, naiyak ang Tita. She can't imagine doing this all over again after losing the husband to sickness. My dear, it's ok to date and meet new people at this age. A lot do it. I have been doing it. Nakakapresure lang talaga kasi we set expectations for ourselves that at this age we should have it all.

Thank you girls for this lovely convo. I miss you all more.

"Diamond"

May kilala akong human na ganito. And I admit, I probably have taken a lot of people for granted. Guilty.

Sabi nga, when someone throws away a diamond, the diamond stays a diamond. It's the one who threw it that makes him/her stupid.

"Pera ko"

R: Di ako makamove sa nawala kong pera.. Paano ba?

C: Isipin mo na lang it was never yours to begin with. Pwede rin ba iapply sa real life yan ate?

Ako pa tinanong ng batang to. Well pwede naman. Mahirap nga lang. Isipin mo na lang he was never yours to begin with? Ay. Hard.

Basta ako now nasasaktan dahil nawalan. Hindi ko pa napapakinabangan nawala na. Buti pa yung lalake napakinabangan muna bago nawala!

"Now you're just a story I tell people when we talk about hurt."

Out of sight, out of mind.
Out of mind, out of heart.

"Let it go. See what kind of magic returns in its place. What's for you will never reach you while you're clinging to something else."

"I understand feeling as small and as insignificant as humanly possible. And how it can actually ache in places you didn't know you had inside you. And it doesn't matter how many new haircuts you get, or gyms you join, or how many glasses of chardonnay you drink with your girlfriends... you still go to bed every night going over every detail and wonder what you did wrong or how you could have misunderstood. And how in the hell for that brief moment you could think that you were that happy." - Iris, The Holiday

"I'll be waiting for you in our next lifetime. Maybe then, we will get this whole thing right."

"Some love stories aren't epic novels — some are short stories. But that doesn't make them any less filled with love."

Never make someone very special in your life, because when they change, you don't hate them. You start hating yourself.

"It's okay... To have a broken heart means that you have tried for something." - Eat, Pray, Love

"Sometimes it's not the person you miss. It's the feeling you had when you were with them."

I thought that I'd been hurt before
But no one's ever left me quite this sore
Your words cut deeper than a knife
Now I need someone to breathe me back to life...

"Feel what you have to feel, then let it go. Don't let it consume you."

"Forgive not because the other needs forgiveness. But because you need peace."

Time flies. Not exactly just when you're having fun, but when you're hurting too.

It's been almost 3 years. I longed and held on for 2. The pandemic has brought something wonderful, and that's to make me detach myself from the craziness of it all.

Your worst enemy is your own memory.

"How do you know when it's over?"
"When you feel more in love with your memories than with the person standing in front of you."

"If I had known then what I knew now, I would have seen the red flag warning signs, but I did not. She was beautiful, seemingly incredibly interested in me and my work, and I fell for it. She bombed me with what appeared to be love."

- Johnny Depp

And in his silence I realized,
I liked him.
Maybe I even loved him.
But that didn't entitle me to have all of him.

"To let you in again and gain so much power over me... I cannot let this happen."

So timely to have read this, just when someone from the past who has left painful memories, has found his way back to my life.
I can't. I won't. You cannot have that power again. Ever.

This goes out to you.

People say differences shouldn't matter when you want things to work out. I'm a believer of this. Laban hanggang dulo. Pero, hanggang saan ang dulo?

Knowing yourself and each other defines that limitation. We were quick to like, eager to love, but not built for it. At least not yet.

Maybe in time, who knows? Maybe in time, we'll know how to be right for each other. Maybe in time, we can love each other the way we want and need to be loved, in the way that we can and know how.

It was great until it wasn't, but no regrets. My heart's tired and in pieces, but still overwhelmed with irreplaceable memories of you. This is not the end for us. Maybe this is the start of something more beautiful that we didn't focus on when we had the chance.

Know that I love you, for who you are and what you will become.

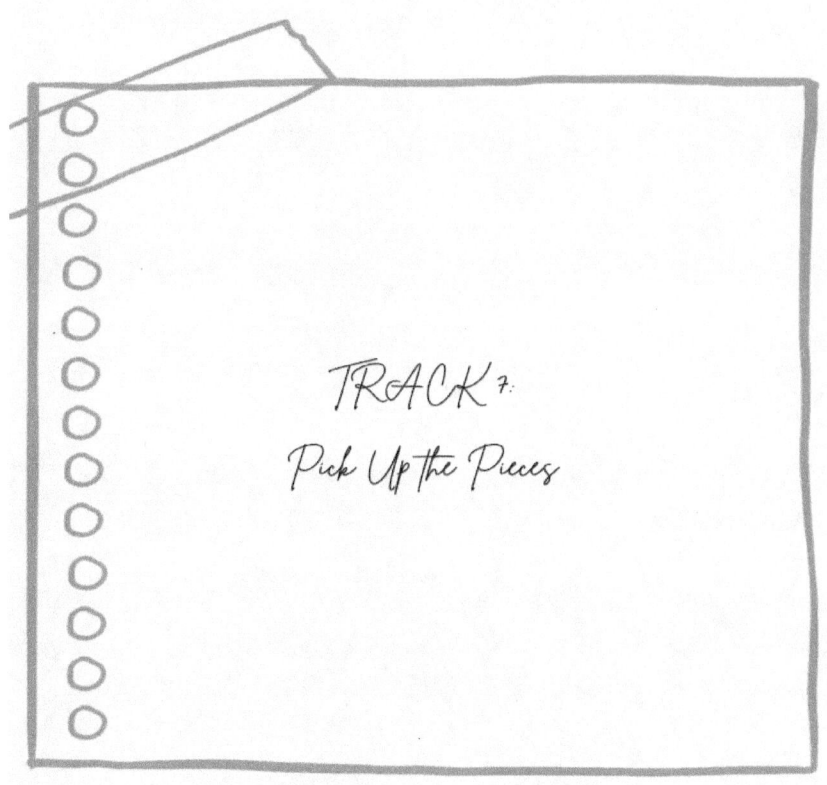

Playlist Companion

You've Made Me Stronger — by Regine Velasquez

Someday by Nina

All The Love In The World by The Corrs

Flowers by Miley Cyrus

All I Know So Far by Pink

Fight Song by Rachel Platten

Who You Are by Jessie J

This Is Me by Keala Settle

Tuloy Pa Rin by Neocolours

Tears by Clean Bandit

"A monie marble is a translucent marble, and I suppose what I like about it is that when a bright light casts a shadow on it there's a distinct fire burning at its center. They have a remarkable inner glow." - The Marble Collector, Cecelia Ahern

Just like the moonie marbles, when something or someone comes to dim our path or cloud our judgement, remember, there is a fire burning at your center, in anything and anyone is something to behold and hone.

Never lose that fire and passion.

"Have that conscious effort to change, until it becomes effortless."

If you want to change something in you, you first have to realize what is wrong (or someone tells you directly). If you agree, then you have to make that conscious effort to change -- be mindful of your words and actions, especially, how they would affect others.

Daily you would find that it will become effortless, that you've changed your ways. You would know because they (or the person who pointed it out) will notice.

But remember, effort to change has to come from within. We have to want to change, to believe we can change...and we're halfway there.

In anything we do, once the effort is shown, it is an indication that we are doing it for something or someone important.

I know.

I just know.

My own version of happiness will come,

Love as I define it will appear,

In the most opportune time.

Someday,

The universe will conspire to bring two souls together.

I know.

"Nakakamiss yung may jowa no? Yung may sasalo ng pagka-bipolar mo."

Be with someone who will take you for who you are -- mood swings, tantrums, rants, issues and all -- not someone who'd turn his back when things get rough and pressure rises.

"Even at your best, you will never be right for the wrong person. But at your worse, the right person will always see your worth." – Shetty

Value those who pulled you from dark times. Appreciate them and their little ways of saving us from the wrong people.

"Giant is Hate. A Giant comes to the place and takes everything from you, and when it's done it's like anything that made your life good was never even there." - I Kill Giants

Oftentimes, we fill our heads with negative thoughts that turn out to affect our actions, how we feel, and how we perceive life in general. It's feeding your heart with hate, the hate grows until it consumes you. When it does, it will be difficult to find joy in everything that surrounds you.

Don't let your giants defeat you. Find it. Hunt it. Kill it. You're stronger than you think.

"Life isn't fair, but it's still good."

I guess what's really missing in most people's lives is the conscious effort to be thankful for every experience good or bad. They all gave us life lessons. I will never understand why some people would want to end their lives when we only have one shot at it.

Let's all just understand what each other is going through. We will never really know what's going on because we are not in the situation.

"Happy. For real."

Still one of the best advice...

"In whatever you decide to do, please don't forget your son, and how he deserves the best mom to him. And you can be the best if you are truly happy and at peace with the decisions that you make."

"When you love someone you protect them from the pain, you don't become the cause of it."

"Integrity"

A good friend once told me, "Integrity: It's either you have it or you don't."

This also goes hand in hand with Honesty and Credibility. It is not fair that you know something that's told to be the truth, and then find out there's an entirely different scenario that was cooked behind your back.

Is it that difficult to be honest these days that we tell lies at the expense of other people?

I guess it's not the "difficulty" of being honest. It's just that there's no embedded integrity to begin with. Again, there is no "sometimes" in integrity.

Another good friend told me, "Ang parinig masakit pag totoo." Hindi ako nagpaparinig. Nag-eexpress lang. Now kung may tamaan, bakit kaya.

"Whatever you're not changing, you are choosing."

"Loved A Little More"

"Isn't everything we do in life a way to be loved a little more?"

Come to think of it, we talk about self-improvement, self-worth, at lahat na ng nagsisimula sa self. But why? So that we can love ourselves more? Kasi self love daw e. The truth is, start lang yung self-love. We must admit, that we do all this self-love thing so that we get to be loved by others more.

Para saan ang ganda kung ikaw lang naman titingin. Para saan ang achievements kung ikaw lang ang nagdiriwang. Para saan ang paghahanda ng sarili at puso kung walang paglalaanan.

Wag na umarte ng "I'm doing this for myself." Lahat ng tao gusto ng pansin, kalinga, at pagmamahal.

"The problem, causes and reasons are with the X. It then affects the Y."

For every problem, there is a solution. You just have to go back to identifying what the causes and reasons are from the X. Then, the Y should decide if it remains unaffected, or if goals have to be adjusted/changed.

"Say No"

"A 'yes' woman who gives too much sends the impression that she believes in the man more than she believes in herself. Men view this as a weakness, not kindness."

Mag-no ka minsan. Kahit one time lang. Balik natin when you were just starting to talk and make head gestures. No naman talaga ang mas nauunang natututunan bago yes.

Buti pa ang toddlers strong ang peg.

"There is more to living than NOT dying."

I've hear this from the movie #TheCroods, and this time from the book #ClockworkPrincess.

The universe is telling me/us something: Live life to the fullest. We've only got ONE chance. Let's make the most of it.

"You will look back and realize that everytime you thought you were being rejected from something good, you were actually being redirected to something better."

"Though my soul may set in darkness, it will rise in perfect light;

I have loved the stars too fondly to be fearful of the night." - Sarah Williams, The Old Astronomer

"Self Love"

"Take a long hard look at what you are worth. The love you attract (and fight for) reflects the value you place on yourself."

Self worth. Always difficult to assess. Siguro basta magpakasmart. Wag pagamit. Wag ding manggamit. E minsan (or madalas) naman sa love, we accept the love we think we deserve.

Pag gusto, gusto. Walang isip isip. O di go. Wag lang aarte sa huli pag napagod sa pambabasura ng iba. Dahil in the first place, he treats you like trash coz that's how you presented yourself to him. That was the value you placed on yourself.

"May Kiliti Ako Dyan"

I saw this one as I was doing my usual fb browsing...

"Bakit pag kiniliti mo sarili mo hindi ka natatawa? Pero pag kiniliti ka ng iba, matatawa ka? Kailangan ba talaga ng ibang tao para sumaya?"

 Depende. Siguro sa larangan ng kilitian e talagang kailangan may ibang tao 'no. Ang lungkot naman na kilitiin mo sarili mo. Lakas naman makabaliw nyan.

Pero, hindi malungkot na pasayahin mo sarili mo. You can make yourself happy even when on your own. Go places. Buy things. Set goals and achieve them. Most of all, accept yourself and be content with what you have.

"Moving forward without honest effort is moving backward in disguise."

"Finders Keepers"

"Malelate ako. Di ko mahanap wallet at sarili ko."

It's difficult when you lose something of value, what more if it's a person or your peace of mind?

Start the search. If it's meant to be found, you will find it. Kung ayaw magpahanap, wag pag aksayahan ng panahon. Kung nanakaw na, gauge if it's worth being back in your life.

"Hope"

This is the ultimate wish: To have someone protect our hearts from any pain.

I guess it just becomes painful when someone already cares less, or loves less for that matter.

Despite all the pain though, I have never given up on love. I will not lose hope.

"They say before something great happens to you, everything falls apart."

"WORTH"

The man described is everything anyone could ever hope for...and everything you're not. But still, I surrender to you...

"You deserve to be with someone who looks at you every single day like he won the lottery and has the whole world in front of him. You deserve someone who can help you reach your dreams and can protect you from your fears. You deserve someone who will treat you with respect and will love every part of you, especially your flaws. You deserve someone who is not ashamed to love you and tells all his friends about you and saves all your selfies, whether they are good or bad, to look at when he misses you. You deserve his attention more than his phone does. You deserve effort and quality time. You deserve to be treated as his topmost priority not the last thing on his checklist. You are special and you deserve to be happy, really happy.

Begging for love is suicide. It's like begging a servant to serve his queen. An injustice, I say, to give your body to a man who wouldn't dare to walk with you in public nor ever consider standing next to you at the altar.

If that's too much to ask, perhaps you are asking from the wrong person. There's someone who can. They exist. I promise."

"You can't win someone who is not afraid to lose you."

"I just realized, maybe it's maturity or the wisdom that comes with age, but the witch in 'Hansel and Gretel'—she's very misunderstood. I mean, the woman builds her dream house and these brats come along and start eating it."

You will always be too much for the wrong person. Too clingy. Too sensitive. Paranoid. Too needy for time and attention. But to the right one, you are enough. More than enough. Without even asking, he will give you things that you truly deserve.

Stop taking them back. You deserve someone who doesn't only want you when they see you happy without them.

"There are people we go through to learn about what love is NOT."

Sad. But true. There would be people who will come into our lives and leave, just so we learn lessons from them. From them, you would realize what you really want in a relationship; what you can take and endure; what you can and can't live without.

But learning takes a while. Minsan nga we never learn at all kahit na ilang daang tao pa ang magturo sa atin.

I say... Willpower and prayers is the key! Pag gusto matuto, matututo. Pag ayaw, then you'd continue believing what you want to believe about love.

So do you want to continue believing that love is painful and that's what you deserve? Think.

"Healing isn't linear. Be gentle with yourself."

"Sometimes it takes losing what you were settling for to remember what you deserve."

"You are not selfish for wanting the same energy and love you give."

Emotions are part of the equation of our lives, but not the entire equation. Just because something feels good doesn't mean it is good. Just because something feels bad doesn't mean it is bad. Emotions are merely signposts, suggestions that our neurobiology gives, not commandments. Therefore, we shouldn't always trust our own emotions. I believe we should make a habit of questioning them.

"I want to be someone's favorite hello and hardest goodbye."

"I wanted the reward and not the struggle. I wanted the result and not the process. I was in love with not the fight but just the victory. And life doesn't work that way."

Most people want a partner. A husband or a wife. But you don't end up attracting someone amazing without appreciating the emotional battles that come with rejections, building the sexual tension that never gets released, and staring blankly at a phone that never rings. It's part of the game of love. You can't win if you don't play. What determines your success isn't, 'What do you want to enjoy?'. The relevant question is 'What pain do you want to sustain?'. The path to happiness is a path full of failures and shame. You have to choose something. You can't have a pain-free life. It can't all be rainbows and unicorns all the time. Pleasure is the easy question. and pretty much all of us have a similar answer.

"Our scars can destroy us. Even after the physical wounds have healed. But if we survive them, they can transform us. They can give us the power to endure and the strength to fight."

Playlist Companion

You Got Me by Colby Caillat

Ikaw Pa Rin by Moira Dela Torre/Erik Santos

I'll Never Not Love You by Michael Buble

Have It All by Jason Mraz

More Today Than Yesterday by The Spiral Staircase

Love Is An Open Door by Kristen Bell/Santino Fontana

Babalik Sa'yo by Moira dela Torre

Gorgeous by Taylor Swift

All I Ask of You by Andrew Lloyd Webber

Could I Love You Any More by Renee Dominique/Jason Mraz

"What If"

From one of the cutest movies, #LettersToJuliet

Dear Claire,

"What" and "If" are two words as non-threatening as words can be. But put them together side-by-side and they have the power to haunt you for the rest of your life: What if? What if? What if? I don't know how your story ended but if what you felt then was true love, then it's never too late. If it was true then, why wouldn't it be true now? You need only the courage to follow your heart. I don't know what a love like Juliet's feels like - love to leave loved ones for, love to cross oceans for but I'd like to believe if I ever were to feel it, that I will have the courage to seize it. And, Claire, if you didn't, I hope one day that you will.

All my love,
Juliet

"It's kinda cool how someone can just pop into your life all of a sudden and become so important to you within such a small amount of time. I think that's what makes life so interesting. There's always a reason to be hopeful for the future because you never know what good things will come your way."

"You should never have to fight for love. If it's love, it will stay."

"Sometimes the right place is a person."

"You later realize that love is no longer about you, but about the person you love."

"Sacrifices"
No one can really know why you would move mountains for someone. Only you can answer that.

"Life is for deep kisses, strange adventures, midnight swims and rambling conversations."

Everything. Every second. Every part of you. Every whisper, hug and kiss. I miss.

"We're different people now. I hope we can meet again for the first time."

**"May love greet you at your door
with hunger in it's eyes,
passion dripping from it's lips,
and loyalty in its touch."**

Someone told me this earlier (you know who you are if you get to read this) while I was ranting about someone's confusing intentions -- **"We all need a little love, and the provider is not always perfect."**

Got me thinking. While it's true, this doesn't mean that settling for less or confusing "little love" is the way to go. No matter how little, it should be sincerely given and reciprocated. "The provider is not always perfect" -- nobody is, but someone is meant to be perfect for another person, flaws and all.

"Choosing to be together -- That is the ultimate recipe for having a healthy relationship."

> "And every heartbreak was a yellow brick road
> Pointing me straight, just taking me home
> I was never lost
> I was just passing through
> I was on my way to you..."

It's special how you find your own beautiful little mess that fits perfectly with you.

"We burn for water, we growl for food. But what we yearn for most is comfort. A soft embrace. Someone to whisper 'It's all right. It's all right'."

True love is attempting to understand the things another person's mind thinks and your mind doesn't; it's being inspired by them. It's wondering how you found someone whose differences complement yours. Differences are normally things that tear people apart, but in true love, your differences bring you closer together. It's like a beautiful little mess and that mess fits perfectly between the cracks inside your heart you never knew how to fill. True love fills those cracks without making you forget that they exist. True love allows you to remember the past and how hard it might have been, and then it allows you to feel grateful for what you have now. True love makes you feel lucky to find it.

FOUND IT

Love. When we're looking for it, we can't find it. Sometimes we even mistake something for love just because we desperately want it to be love. We chase it like crazy only to find out it wasn't worth it.

And then unexpectedly, in God's perfect timing, the universe gives us love -- or makes us realize that it's been there all this time.

Maybe love found me again and I feel blessed and grateful.

DAYDREAMS

Sometimes she lies awake dreaming
Of a time when hearts didn't question and hearts didn't break
Feeling too much, falling too fast, loving too soon
Moments when scars didn't need much tending
Didn't need much time healing
A time when she knew exactly what love was
Beach strolls and sunsets
Butterfly kisses, leaping heartbeats
Senseless conversations that made the most sense
A series of nothings worth more than many somethings
As the day turns into night unknowingly
She lies awake dreaming
Of how much time has slipped
Like sand between her fingers
Is she living a small life? A valuable one?
Moments of dreaming with eyes open
Made her wonder and realize
She lives a life of irreplaceable adventure
One filled with unconditional love
A love beyond measure and will never ask for anything in return

She lives in a world of magic
A realm of simple pleasures and hurts that defined her
Tight hugs, swift kisses, touches that wake the senses
Happiness and heartbreaks that linger
Moments of love found, lost, and found again
Is it a small life? She would often ask. Did she make the most of it?
Maybe, but it is valuable to many, no doubt
For that she will change nothing
She would do everything over again if she could
Her heart is still strong enough to take the beatings and blessings
She won't stop dreaming and continue doing
Wait patiently for wondrous things yet to unfold
As time goes ticking by, slowly, and then quickly
She is awake and blessed to live more, be more
Eager to live bolder, love better, and dream bigger.

AFTERWORD

Some would say that love is one of the most important human emotions. You are all witnesses now that I have experienced

characteristics of love in different ways…intimacy, passion,

commitment, care, closeness, protectiveness, attraction, affection, and trust.

Many say "It's not an emotion in the way we typically understand them, but an essential physiological drive".

However you define it, it's how it made you feel and made you "human" that matters.

Who knows there might be a sequel to this randomness. For now, I end this compilation with a famous quote that I truly believe:

"It is better to have loved and lost, than not to have loved at all." - Alfred Tennyson

About the Author

REi AGUSTIN

Rei is a Psychology graduate and single mom from Manila, Philippines. She is a nature lover, coffee enthusiast, and a fan of Young Adult fiction novels. She is a wide reader with an ever-growing collection of books. She entertains her addiction by spending time in bookstores or online book groups.

When she is not reading, Rei spends most of her time in the theaters watching musicals, writing, visiting malls, and trying out new cafes and restaurants with her family and friends.

She aspires to write more. After all, experiences are constant and inspiration is endless.

www.ingramcontent.com/pod-product-compliance
Lightning Source LLC
LaVergne TN
LVHW041951070526
838199LV00051BA/2984